THREE AT SEA

Timothy Bush

CROWN PUBLISHERS, INC., NEW YORK

For my parents,
who let us bring home
every kind of animal
known to man

Alex, Joel, and Zachariah Jr. went floating on the river.

Alex was thinking about joining the navy. Joel was thinking about pushing Alex in. Zachariah Jr. was thinking about animals. He was trying to remember if it was alligators that had long, pointed snouts and crocodiles that had rounded ones, or if it was the other way around. He had read it in a book once and now he wasn't sure.

Mostly, though, they were thinking about nothing in particular and let the water carry them wherever it went.

Where it went was out to sea.

"Bad," said Alex.

"Scary," said Joel.

"Precarious," said Zachariah Jr., and the other two hit him for using long words.

They asked some passing sea turtles for a ride to shore, but the turtles said they never went that far.

"Got to be careful," they said. "After all, we're endangered, you know."

"At the moment," said Alex, "so are we."

But the turtles swam off, so Alex said,
"Selfish."
And Joel said, "Piggy."
Zachariah Jr. said, "I can't blame them,"
and the other two had to hit him again.

They tried to make a sail out of Joel's
red bandanna, but there wasn't any wind,
and a pair of dolphins laughed at them.
"You could give us a hand instead of
laughing," Alex yelled.

"It's no good," said Zachariah Jr. "We've made them endangered and now they're too rare to help us."

"Oh, they're useless," said Alex. "Unless we can use them for food or something."

"Funny you should say that," said a dark voice behind them. "I was just thinking the same thing about you . . ."

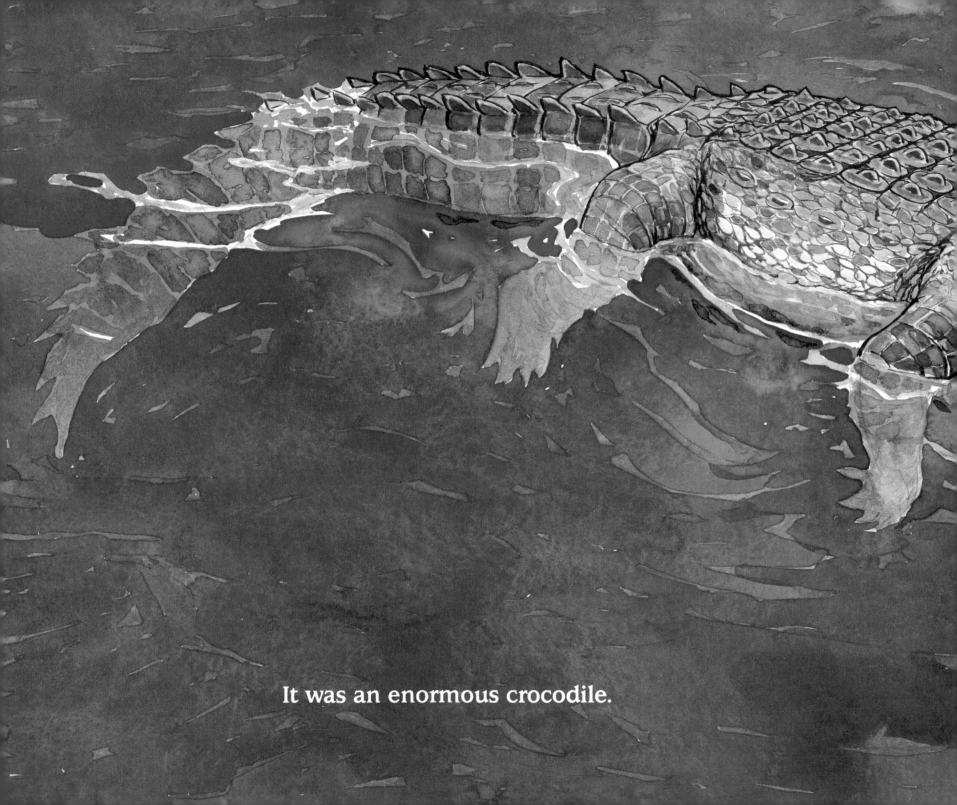

It was an enormous crocodile.

"Urp," said Alex.

"Gak," said Joel.

"Are you an alligator or a crocodile?" asked Zachariah Jr. "I can never remember which one is which."

"Alligator?" The crocodile stopped in mid-bite. "*Alligator*?!
With a long, pointed snout like this? Are you *joking*?!"

"I'm just *asking*," said Zachariah Jr. "So the alligator is the one with the short, rounded snout?"

"Short, rounded, and *ugly*," snapped the crocodile. "An alligator's got a face like a *shovel*. Look!"

It stuck its face into Zachariah Jr.'s so he could see how long and elegant it really was.

Before the crocodile could pull away, Zachariah Jr. tied up its snout with Joel's red bandanna.

The crocodile was furious. He rolled in the water and wiggled and splashed, trying to shake the bandanna loose.

In the end, it didn't help. Crocodiles have powerful muscles for snapping their jaws *shut*, but the muscles used for *opening* them are much, much weaker. This knowledge and a good knot in the red bandanna put Zachariah Jr. in charge of the situation.

"We'd like to go home, please," he said . . .

. . . and the crocodile had to take them.

They pulled the bandanna off from the safety of the dock. Alex said they ought to leave it on, but the others said the crocodile had to eat. After all, it was endangered, too.

The crocodile was not as grateful as it might have been.

Alex and Joel stayed over that night. They fell asleep early, but Zachariah Jr. sat up till eleven writing letters to the president about taking better care of the animals.

ABOUT
THE ANIMALS
IN
THIS BOOK:

SEA TURTLES live almost entirely in the water, coming ashore only to lay their eggs. It is at this time that they are most vulnerable, hunted sometimes for food but mostly for their shells, which are made into a wide variety of products or simply sold as tourist souvenirs. Since sea turtles nest in the same place year after year, protecting these areas has been important in turtle conservation.

DOLPHINS are among the most intelligent animals in the world. Although they spend their entire lives in the water, they are mammals, not fish, and are related to whales. They are threatened in many areas by commercial fishing.

CROCODILES are the largest living reptiles and look today much as they did in the time of the dinosaurs. Fully grown, they have no enemies but man; still, hunting and habitat loss have greatly reduced their numbers worldwide. Most crocodiles do not usually swim in the open ocean, but several species— including the American crocodile—are sometimes found in salt water, pulled out to sea by tides and storms.

HUMAN BEINGS are part of the animal kingdom, too. (Well, think about it; you're not a plant, are you?)

To find out more, ask your librarian or local bookseller.

Published by Crown Publishers, Inc., a Random House company, 201 East 50th Street, New York, New York 10022
CROWN is a trademark of Crown Publishers, Inc.

Manufactured in the United States of America

Library of Congress Cataloging-in-Publication Data
Bush, Timothy.
Three at Sea / by Timothy Bush
p. cm.
Summary: When three boys accidentally float downriver and out to sea on an inner tube, they look for help from several endangered animals.
[1. Rare animals—Fiction. 2. Rivers—Fiction. 3. Adventure and adventurers—Fiction.] I. Title.
PZ7.B96545Th 1994
[E]—dc20   93-3677

ISBN 0-517-59299-1

10 9 8 7 6 5 4 3 2 1   First Edition